THE HEIR

NANA MALONE

CHAPTER ONE

SAFFRON

I DUCKED a wild swing and then kicked my foot out, hitting my target center mass.

Next to me on the training mats, my best mate and teammate for this exercise, Tabatha Smith, panted happily as she clotheslined her sparring partner.

When he went down like a sack of potatoes, hacking, coughing, and clutching his throat, she grinned at me.

I couldn't help but laugh. Unfortunately, in the second that I took my eyes off my target, I caught a fist straight to the sternum.

People always said that they got the wind knocked out of them, but this was a whole other kind of thing. Not only was the wind knocked out of me, my sparring partner was six-foot-five, 250 pounds. And he had not pulled his punch.

I got my soul and my sass knocked out of me.

I had, of course, been trained on what to do when you had no air and you still had to fight for your life.

I whipped my leg out and caught him behind the knee, pitching him forward. He fell down, and I quickly rolled on top of him as I took a large breath. Then I delivered a hammer fist right to the center of his chest, making him cough.

Somewhere in the distance a whistle blew, and I immediately sprang up to my feet, making a point to pretend like I wasn't breathing hard. But dear God, I didn't think I'd ever breathe deeply again.

Tabatha smirked at me. "You know you're going to get docked for control, right?"

I glowered at the trainee still laying on his back and smirked. "It was worth it." I leaned over him, smiling softly. "Trainee, control, remember?"

He grumbled from where he lay, still coughing. "Sorry."

He nodded, as if accepting the reprimand. But in his eyes I could see the challenge, the desire to put me back in my place, and I knew he'd be a problem as an op who needed to follow orders in the field. Not that he couldn't be an op, but teamwork was going to be an issue for him.

The trainees were given their marks for the day, and they all shuffled and filed out toward the locker rooms. Tabatha threw her arm over my shoulder. "Okay, now that work is done for the day, please, can we go celebrate your damn birthday?"

I wrinkled my nose. "My birthday isn't until tomorrow."

"Oh, come on. You know I'm off for three days straight. If we don't celebrate until tomorrow, I'll have wasted a night of freedom. And if we celebrate tonight, you and I can still get out of here and go to the city for the weekend."

"You know full well I can't go anywhere."

She frowned. "Sir Gabe won't let you out of the tower, huh?"

I groaned. Gabriel Webb was our commander. He was also my adopted brother and in charge of my schedule. Basically, he was in charge of *me* because of how things had landed over the last two years.

"Come on, it's your *birthday*. Even Gabe can't keep you from that."

He could. He would, too.

"It doesn't matter how mad he is, okay? I just don't want to do anything wild or crazy." Despite being so close, Tabatha and I were exact opposites. She loved the energy of a loud, bustling club. I did not. I always felt out of place. Like it was too loud. Too hard to see.

She sighed and planted her hands on my shoulders. Tabs was several inches shorter than me, but she was built. Completely stacked in all the areas I was *not*. Tabatha had curves that basically screamed, *Look at me. Watch me.*

I was more gently curved. Athletic. Tall. Not quite willowy, but never would my curves say, *Va-va-va-voom.*

Tabs just laughed. "Come on. You have to have a birthday celebration. It's important to celebrate these things even if you're sad."

Just the mention of it made my nose tingle. "I know.

It's important." After all, hadn't the therapist said the same thing? She'd said it was time to start living my life again.

Easier said than done, but I had to try.

Tabs gave me a soft smile. "No one said you have to become a socialite. I'm just saying a night of dancing with your bestie might make you smile a little."

My parents' death two years ago had scarred me in ways that I would never recover from, but letting my big brother lock me away for my own safety wasn't the answer. "Okay, we'll go out, but nothing crazy, all right?"

Tabatha clapped her hands in glee and jumped up and down. "Yes! Bust out the leather pants because we are doing this birthday right!"

"You are way too excited for this," I grumbled.

Tabs gyrated all around me, and I couldn't help but giggle. "If those are your dance moves, I worry about your sanity."

"You worry about your own moves. Who knows? Maybe we'll even find you someone to shag."

"Nope. Some random sweaty bloke in a bar?" Just the idea made me shudder. "No thanks. Besides, I'm not dating right now."

"We're going to have so much fun. There's a new bar in Mayfair. We're going to go to and let the rich billionaire playboys and sons of the aristocracy buy us stupidly expensive drinks. And then, we're going to head down to South London. I know of a few clubs down there, and one of them is owned by Jamal Winston. He's that Jamaican DJ I was telling you about. He is wicked. I cannot wait."

I snorted. "Tabs, why do I have a feeling that I'm going to need to carry a weapon tonight?"

"When are you ever without a weapon?"

I frowned at that. "Well, that's just good safety. And you should always carry one too."

She shrugged. "I do. But the point is, I feel like you have six whereas I have two."

I blinked rapidly. "Well, you never know when you're going to need a spare."

She lifted her brows while still managing to roll her eyes at me.

I huffed, "All right, fine, I recognized how that sounded when I said it."

"I get it. You are warrior goddess supreme. I adore you. And I don't know how to say this, but you need some dick. All work and no play is very bad for both of us. But especially for you. Time for The Heir to get the cobwebs out."

I loathed my call sign. It was just an ever-present reminder that my parents weren't here.

I shook my head. "Tabs."

I glanced around, hoping none of the other trainers were around, only to realize that we were alone. Gabe hadn't even stayed to get my opinion on the trainees, which meant I would have to go to him. Was that a power play?

Before my parents died, we'd been thick as thieves. But the moment they were gone, he'd changed. He'd become cold, distant, exacting. He'd also gotten a little wild about my safety.

Tabs snorted, the little sound bringing me out of my

reverie. "I love how we're both looking for him but for completely different reasons."

I rolled my eyes. "Please Tabs, I beg you, do not tell me all the dirty things you want to do to my brother."

"He's a pain in the arse, but he's a *hot* pain in the arse."

I shuddered. "That's gross. He's just Gabe."

She gave me a wicked grin and waggled her eyebrows. "Yes, he is *Gabe*. Those broad shoulders... I've watched him train. Shirtless, all sweaty, six-pack abs. That man is fine. How you don't see it, is beyond me."

I wasn't blind. I knew Gabe was a looker. I just also had a front row seat to all his flaws. But he was the only person in the world I fully trusted, and that was saying a lot. I loved Tabs to pieces, but sometimes I didn't trust her decisions or the risks she took. I'd trust Gabe with my life, though I resented the fact that he wouldn't let me out in the field.

"Look, I already agreed to go out with you tonight, so there's no reason to gross me out."

She giggled. "All right, fine, I will keep my lecherous thoughts to myself, but that man is scorching hot."

"So gross."

"He's so fit. But it's not like he would ever look at me that way. Every time he does, he's irritated about it."

I frowned at that. Tabs was stunning. If she had insecurities, what hope was there for us mere mortals? And if Gabe ever did date, hell if he ever left his office, Tabs would be good for him. She was just the sunshine he needed. Not to mention she was great in the field, amazing at hand-to-hand, and distracting for her opponent at the very least. But rumor was, when she'd been a trainee, she had turned down a senior member of the Oversight, some lecherous old fart who'd thought she needed to test out her honey ops training.

And while the Oversight member couldn't sack her exactly, he could make it so she never got to go on any serious ops. Gabe was in the middle of that. I knew it was a source of frustration and a sore spot for her, so I didn't say anything.

"Tabs, what do you always tell me about what we put out into the universe?"

She shook her head stubbornly. "You're right. Time to put out the let's-get-laid energy."

The thing was, I could see it… Tabs and Gabe as a couple. But I knew Gabe was by the book. He would never, *ever* cross that line with her, not when there was a no-fraternization rule in place. As long as she was an operative under his command, he would never touch her. So maybe it was better that her secret attraction for him stayed that way.

Once we were in the locker room, Tabs grabbed her bag and turned to me. "Don't bother getting in the shower, we're going to go straight to yours."

"Why? I can just shower and change here."

She shook her head. "You are *not* putting on the usual costume. Black leggings, black shirt, burgundy leather jacket. That's not an *outfit*. You have clothes. You're wearing them."

I frowned at my bag. "What's wrong with my outfits?"

"They're fine. You know, for the daytime. But we're out to catch some dick, so *you* are going to get a little bit out of your comfort zone."

I frowned at that. "Why on earth does that worry me?"

"Because you and I both know you're hot. And for once, you're not going to think about what the safe thing to do is, what the right thing to do is. We're going to have a little fun because it's your birthday and you fucking deserve it. Now shake a leg. We are going out tonight."

She had a good point. It was my birthday. I deserved to celebrate.

And definitely get laid.

CHAPTER TWO
LACHLAN

I honestly should have ignored the pounding at my door two hours ago. That would have saved me from the thrumming, incessant dance beat I was presently being subjected to.

But my mate Felix had always known how to coax me out. He'd been Charlie's best mate. When my brother died, he'd made me his unofficial little brother.

It didn't matter how many times I tried to remind him I did not need looking after. It wasn't like he ever listened. Felix was a mountain, basically the size of an ape. And he didn't just sit on your shoulder. He liked to latch himself onto your whole back.

He shoved a glass at me. "Drink up, mate."

I glowered at the scotch. He had a point. I'd been in a mood for the past week, ever since the last board meeting. I'd taken one of Charlie's subsidiaries and sold it off. The company had been bleeding money, so I'd sold it off and used the funds for a nonprofit charity in his name. I may or may not have celebrated my coup with a certain Hollywood starlet... by naked kite surfing. My father had been less than pleased.

He'd put me on ice for daring to make decisions without his explicit approval, and now I was being punished. He hadn't exactly stripped me of my title, but he'd assigned me to publicity duty for King Media, a job that didn't matter. All because I'd dared to think for myself.

He knew I hated publicity duty, being trotted out like a prized pony. That's what made the job the perfect punishment. The real question was how long I'd be forced to endure it.

"Drink up, young Padawan. You might even have some fun."

"Felix, give it a rest. I'm not in the mood, mate. Besides, I'm supposed to be laying low, remember? New face of King Media and all that shit."

"Fair enough. But you don't actually want to be the PR lackey, do you? Fuck, mate, live a little."

You didn't have to follow him out tonight.

Except Felix was *that* mate. The one who, no matter what happened, if he called you went, because when you needed him, he was there for you. So I'd come, even though it was against my better judgment.

"Couldn't you have picked somewhere more low-key though?" I wasn't exactly in the mood for a boisterous club.

He shrugged. "You sound like Alyssa. She begged off. Said I was partying too much for her."

I blinked in surprise. Alyssa was his girlfriend of three years. She might not like to party, but she was indulgent when Felix did. Which was often. Whenever there was an adventure, Alyssa was with us. I was convinced that she tempered more of his wilder instincts. "Oh, so you were bored and called me?"

"I'm not bored. I have other mates. It's just you're my *best* mate. Besides, you haven't been out in a week."

"Mate, I'm in no..." Out of the corner of my eye, I caught sight of a woman. Tiny, with reddish-auburn hair that fell in a tumble of curls around her shoulders. Her mate was the exact opposite.

She was tall, dark skinned, and had long braids that cascaded to her hips. Her curves were more subtle but still enough that her arse would fill my hands.

But it was her face that had me completely tuning out Felix and the harsh music. Her neck was long and delicate, and she held it like a dancer. Her cheekbones looked like they were sculpted by a master. Her lips were almost too full for her face. Full enough to give me dirty fantasies in my mind of just what her mouth could do.

But it was her eyes that really held me rooted. In the quick once-over she made of the crowd, her gaze told me so much. She was intelligent, assessing, and she'd seen too much despite being so young.

I had no idea who she was but one glance, one look, and she'd already eviscerated any active brain cells.

Naturally, instead of sensing the imminent danger to my soul, I wanted... more.

Felix glanced around. "Mate, what the fuck are you looking at? Oh. I see. Damn, she's well fit. Tits enough for two handfuls."

I frowned at him, ready to tell him to shut his mouth when I realized he was talking about the wrong girl. "No, not the short one. Her mate."

True to form, Felix laughed. "Mate, she looks too smart for you. Like she can detect bullshit from a mile away."

"Don't give a fuck. She will be mine."

CHAPTER THREE

SAFFRON

"Come on sweetheart, get your shots in. You're staying with me tonight, so no excuses," Tab roared over the noise.

I rolled my eyes. "I'm not going to do shots."

"Yes, you are. You need to loosen up."

"I'm plenty loose," I said stiffly. But I wasn't. I knew I should try to relax and have some fun. It was my bloody birthday after all.

Tabitha laughed. "Honey, you're clutching onto your phone like it's your lifeline out of hell. We don't get service in hell, babes."

I had to laugh at that. "Okay, fine. I will relax." She was right. Having fun wouldn't kill me.

She handed me a shot. I didn't even bother asking what it was. It was my birthday. I could live a little.

"Hottie hunt time!"

"Tabs, I'm not hooking up with some random bloke."

"Love, when was the last time you hooked up with *any* bloke, random or otherwise?"

I tried not to think about my last disastrous attempt at any kind of hookup. I was starting to believe that I wasn't really cut out for hooking up. I needed to know someone. I needed to actually like them as a person. Yes, I had had sex. But my last attempts had been awkward, and there was certainly no magic. No amazing orgasms. No orgasms at all for that matter. The guy had been fine. I just hadn't particularly enjoyed myself, and all I wanted to do was to get rid of him. But he was that kind of bloke who holds on tight afterward. And then he wanted to go a second round. I had to leave my own flat just to escape him.

Luckily, that had been in uni, so Gabe hadn't had constant security on me. Maybe that was part of the reason I didn't date. I was always expecting my brother to be somewhere around the corner ready to ruin my life. I tried to find the spirit of fun as we shoved our way through the club, and Tabs took my hand as soon as a song from Three Six Mafia came on. All I heard was a roar of women as everyone ran for the dance floor, making it a packed, sweaty, sex gyration.

I normally didn't like crowds or that closed-in feeling. But this was fine because there was dancing involved and I could close my eyes and be someone else.

As Tabs and I danced and the songs switched easily from Three Six Mafia to Dua Lipa to Britney Spears and then to Sean Paul, I moved my body in time with the music, rocking my hips.

I'd always loved to dance. I got it from my mother. When I was dancing, I could be anybody. I could hide. I could pretend.

Or maybe you are showing your true self.

Tabs and I had gathered a small audience as we worked through different dance styles. We took it from the 80's to present, laughing our way through the silliness. The twerking and wining were the crowd favorites.

As I danced, I mostly kept my eyes closed, just letting my body move to the music. Suddenly, mid twirl, I could feel a prickle of awareness. My eyes blinked open and I searched the crowd. I knew people were watching, but I didn't care. It was my birthday, and I wasn't going to do some strained, quiet dinner with Gabe where he gave me some present that had nothing to do with who I was. Being out. Being free. Friends, dancing. Fun. This was what I needed. I told myself I was being paranoid. Yes, men were watching, but there was no danger here. Except that feeling, the prickly heat sensation, moved from my neck to my limbs, and the hairs on my arms stood at attention.

Someone was watching me.

I danced and turned in a circle, looking for who was causing me the heightened fight reflex.

That's not a fight reflex. That's a fuck reflex.

My gaze flickered over a bloke who was about five-foot-ten and blond, and he took that as an invitation.

His mate wrapped his hands around Tab's waist, pulling her into him. She smiled coyly at him as she turned around to get a good look at his face. The blond bloke started dancing closer to me, but the look I gave him probably terrified him because he did not touch me, which was in his best interest.

I knew he wasn't the bloke who had been staring at me because I still felt the kiss of hyperawareness and the tantalizing tug of adrenaline. *Fight or fuck.*

The four of us danced. Tabs with her bloke, and me in the vicinity of the blond. The intensity grew as my breath rate increased. This was a flight response, a warning. More on edge now, I was less surreptitious about seeking out the source. Was there a problem? Was there danger? Was I paranoid? My instincts said no.

My mother told me to never ignore that feeling. To always pay attention to my instincts and what they were telling me. She taught me not to react to it before taking in all of the information.

Then I saw him. The man was watching from one of the booths. He was in the VIP section talking with another man who had a girl with blond hair and big fake boobs on his lap. She had big hair, extensions, the whole bit. Almost like she was a caricature of herself. He caught me looking his way, and our gazes held and locked. Then the barest hint of a smile tipped up the corner of his lip. He wore a long-sleeved white button down with the sleeves rolled up, showing off muscular forearms. His hair was artfully tousled as if he'd just run gel through it haphazardly. I could tell it was dark, curling slightly. He had on dark jeans. Maybe black. On one of his hands, he wore two rings. Silver or platinum, maybe. No visible tattoos that I could see. He wore something around his neck. I couldn't make out the design of the pendant, but it wasn't on a metallic chain. Maybe it was leather or something else.

I purposefully angled my body away, dancing and turning my back to him just to make sure I wasn't imagining it. When I turned back to him, his gaze hadn't faltered.

It was pinned on me. He cocked his head as if asking what I was doing. His half smile deepening to show a hint of a dimple.

He'd seen me watching him, watching me, as if I was going to go over there and talk to him. He must be used to that. Given the VIP booth and the expensive but understated clothing, he was absolutely used to that. He understood power and expected to wield it. Well, he was going to be disappointed.

My dance partner must have seen the direction of my gaze because he angled his body to block my view. And then he tried to start talking to me. "So, uh, you and your mate, you come here often?"

I blinked up at him in surprise, not sure I'd heard correctly. "Sorry, what did you say?"

I glanced at Tabs and the way she was snogging the other bloke, and I figured they'd be off to shag soon.

He reached his hand back and rubbed the back of his neck. "You've been acting a bit stuck up. You're not talking to me."

Was he serious? Maybe it was time to get another drink. "I'm just dancing. That's all."

"Do you want to sit down somewhere and talk?"

Talking was absolutely the last thing I wanted to do. "No, I'm just going to continue dancing. You go ahead though if you're tired."

He frowned. "Well, you know, I thought we'd get to know each other better. Come on, we'll get some privacy."

I shook my head. "No. I'm good."

He narrowed his eyes. "You're a bloody tease, practically showing me your arse. But now when I want to go somewhere and actually, I don't know, buy you a drink and talk to you, you're blowing me off?"

I forced my tone to be neutral and unemotional. "I want you to hear me very clearly, whatever the hell your name is, and understand me. No is a full sentence. I'm not interested. Find someone else who is." Then I very deliberately turned my back on him. All the while, during our little conversational exchange, our bodies had rotated so the bloke in the booth could see us. Except when I looked back over, he was gone.

My dancing partner shook his head and scowled, but he didn't leave. I prayed he didn't become a problem.

Not that I couldn't handle a problem, but problems were messy. I executed another quick turn and was disappointed to find my man in the booth still gone. I couldn't explain the sinking feeling I had in my stomach, the wash of disappointment and the prickle of sadness that he wasn't there. I told myself it was just disappointment because it had felt nice. I'd liked the way he looked at me. Finally, blond bloke sulked off. Good riddance. But Tabs had dragged his mate to our booth, so I couldn't go back there.

"You handled him easily enough."

I startled and turned slowly because I knew without a doubt who was behind me. When I glanced up at him, he quirked his lips in a smile. "I saw you watching me."

I lifted my brow. "You were watching me first."

"Are you sure? Or did I merely return your very direct stare."

I laughed. "Are you shitting me? You were giving off serious creeper vibes. I almost walked over to give you a pair of binoculars."

"My eyesight is excellent. Luckily, I did not need them. It was easy enough to spot the most striking woman in the room."

I rolled my eyes. "Is there a reason you're staring at me?"

He gave me a broader smile then, and my stomach flipped, and the awareness changed into something else. A crackling electric tension. He was even more beautiful up close. His eyes were a startling, silvery, gray with thick, sooty lashes. His jawline and cheekbones screamed for their own magazine cover. And his lips... Well, they had a slightly swollen quality that suggested they might have recently been kissed.

He was the kind of handsome you see in magazines and movies, not the kind of handsome you see walking around romancing all the people.

He was also tall. Enormous actually. I was five foot

eight, and he *towered* over me, so much so that I had to tilt my chin very deliberately to meet that silvery gaze. His eyes were so vibrant. To top off the Greek god façade, he had a cleft in his chin. It really wasn't fair. Under normal circumstances, I would not have stood a chance.

But tequila was bringing out my sass. "You do think highly of yourself, don't you?"

The grin was back, and I saw another flash of dimple. Oh, hell. This bloke was the kind of beautiful you only dream about.

He shook his head. "Everyone should know what they're working with, as I'm sure you do."

I laughed. "Oh, flattery. You know, under normal circumstances, it would get you somewhere."

He cocked his head. "Flattery is not going to get me anywhere?"

"No. It's not. Good try though."

He lifted a brow. "So what do you say? Are you going to actually let me dance with you, or will I be relegated to your last dance partner's status of dancing near you while trying not to look creepy as I try to inch closer and possibly rub up against you?"

I threw my head back and laughed. "Oh my God, you saw that?"

"It was hard to watch. That man did not know how to treat a woman. I'm going to save myself the scarring pain of it all and just simply ask you if you're going to let me dance with you."

I assessed him. My belly was doing that flip-flop thing,

but my belly was a liar. How many times had I had this feeling? That pleasant, amazing feeling of that first attraction when you feel all tingly, and your skin hums, and your lady parts warm, and you are thinking all systems are a go. Only to be insanely disappointed later when go time becomes show time and you are like, 'Oh God, please, God, no.' Still though, I liked the buzz. I liked the feeling of it. The way his lopsided smile made my skin tingle.

I liked the way he was looking at me because I wasn't normally the woman men looked at like that.

Under normal circumstances, I was surrounded by men twenty-four seven. And if even one of them looked at me like that, my brother would shut that shit down quick and send him on a mission he would never return from. But this bloke, he was someone I did not know. He knew nothing about me and just wanted to dance. And dance, I could do. Because dancing was the promise. Even if the execution was always weak, I *loved* the promise. The promise of fun and excitement and orgasms and laughter. I liked the promise above all. "Can you even dance?"

He grinned. "Well, you know, there's only one way to find out. And hey, I'll even do you a solid. I won't actually touch you. You can touch me anywhere you want though."

I laughed, albeit uneasily. How had he already seen all of that? "What do you mean?"

"You seem like the kind of girl who deserves for me to earn the right to touch you. So why don't we dance for a bit? You can touch me all you want."

His observance was doing things to my equilibrium and

that weren't fair because he looked like the kind of person who would be amazing for something fun and easy and uncomplicated.

But my life would always be complicated.

Looking up at his easy smile, I felt myself nodding. I didn't even know why. I knew that this would only lead to disappointment, but it was my birthday and I wanted twenty-two to feel normal. I wanted twenty-two to feel like I could pretend for a moment that I was like everyone else. I could lean into the promise even if I wasn't going to deliver on it.

I glanced up at him. "All right. Just why do you think I'm going to touch you?"

His tongue peeked out to moisten his lower lip, and I couldn't help but stare because... Jesus. He stepped toward me. Close, but not too close. I had room to maneuver. Room to run.

True to his word, he did not put his hands on me. But his eyes never left mine. And as I placed my hands on the firm, packed muscle of his chest I could have sworn I heard the intake of his breath. Sharp. Subtle.

And then we moved together.

When he spoke, his breath tickled my neck. "I knew you would be mine."

CHAPTER FOUR

SAFFRON

Those two inches between us were equal parts a chasm and a magnet we fought against. Or at least *I* fought against it. He kept his word and let me touch him without touching me.

Nervous, I forced my hand to stay on the center of his chest, but then his voice washed over me. That low mellow tone felt like Spanish coffee on a cold day and was hard to ignore as he whispered, "Eyes on me, gorgeous."

I was lost. Honest to God. He might as well have taken what was left of my panties and shredded them because, dear God, I was desperate for him to touch me.

His gaze searched mine. And then he gave me that lopsided smile again. "If you want me to touch you, you're going to have to ask."

I blinked up in surprise. "What do you mean?"

"You keep looking at me like you're waiting for me to do something, but I'm not that arsehole you were dancing with earlier. So if you want me to touch you, you are going to have to ask me to."

His voice was a low rumble, and I could *feel* every word, every syllable, every fragment, deep down under my skin, breaking down on a molecular level to fuse with my cells.

God, that was a good voice.

It was a wake-up-in-the-morning-having-a-gorgeous-man-in-your-bed kind of voice, and he was talking to me like that in the middle of a crowded club where I had to lean in even closer just to hear him.

All I could do was nod and whisper, "You can touch me." I wasn't sure what possessed me to say the words, what possessed me to give my permission. But then he hooked his thumbs in the belt loops of my jeans and pulled my hips in close to him, his gaze never leaving mine. I swallowed hard as the tingling started low in my belly. Holy Christ, I was aroused. The dull, insistent ache between my thighs refused to abate.

With his fingers molded slightly around my waist, just at the upper curve of my arse, he pulled me in even closer, sliding his leg between both of mine. He started to move us to the beat of music, and oh my God.

My pulse throbbed and my blood hummed. For the first time, I got it. I understood. I fully recognized why people made horrible decisions when it came to love and sex and who they should be with. It wasn't clinical. It wasn't something they did by choice. It was instinct. It was something they did because of a low tingle in their vajayjays.

Women across time had made decisions based on this feeling. And I finally got it. I understood.

He leaned in close, his whisper just above my ear. "Is this okay?"

All I could do was nod. God, if only I had been blessed with the gift of saying the right thing at the right moment to seem sexy and interesting and compelling. If only I was Tabs. But no, I had nothing. I had no words to offer instead of staring at him, trying to find something to say.

He gave me a dimple popping grin. "You make me a little nervous too."

I cocked my head then. "What exactly are you reading as nervous?"

He lifted his brow then. "It's the furtive way you look at me and the way you chew on the corner part of your lip. It's been driving me insane since I came over here. It's the way you're holding yourself so stiffly even though our bodies are pressed firmly against each other and you can no doubt feel how much I want you right now and you aren't backing away. So something tells me you like it. You are nervous and terrified, and I completely understand the feeling because you look like you are probably the kind of trouble I don't need."

"Wait, you're saying *I* look like trouble? Hardly. Clearly you've seen a mirror, right?"

He chuckled then. "I own one or two."

"Right. So, I also know someone like you doesn't really need someone like me. You could have any woman in here."

His brow quirked. "You could have any man, but you are dancing with me."

"Hardly. Something about me usually puts men off." He was still watching me like I was the only woman in the room.

"Who was the twat?"

"The wingman. My mate is over there somewhere making out with his friend, so he assumed he was getting lucky too. He was mistaken."

"Can't fault his taste though."

I could feel a hot flush snaking up my neck to my face. I figured that was probably a line, but I felt special, nonetheless. My phone buzzed in my back pocket, and he smiled down at me. "Saved by the bell. Why don't you get that."

I swallowed hard as I reached onto my back pocket, my fingertips grazing his. His fingers flexed on my flesh just a little bit, making me ache in places I didn't know I *could* ache. I glanced down at the phone and saw it was time check protocol. If I didn't call Gabe within the next thirty seconds, he was going to send a detail to my location. "I have to take this outside. It's too loud in here. Will you be here when I get back?"

I hated the sound of my voice, the hope. But if I didn't say something, I knew chances were he'd be dancing with someone who looked more like Tabs. And I definitely wanted to let him know I was coming back.

"Ditching me already?"

"I'm just... Oh, I'll be right back."

He grinned at me. "I'll be right here."

The way he said it was like he said it a lot. Like he was completely at ease saying something like that which meant he would not be here when I came back. Which was fine, because just the act of dancing with him was a religious experience. And that thing he did with his fingers, the way he pulled me in, my God. I was probably pregnant, and Gabe sensed it. Extrasensory perception. That had to be it.

I fought my way through the crowd of packed bodies. When I shoved outside, I went around the corner to avoid the long line of girls scowling at me as they rocked back and forth from foot to foot on the cobblestones in their spindly little heels, rocking miniskirts and crop tops.

I initiated the time check courtesy call and tapped in my code. "This is the Heir, checking in at 11:45 pm."

The dispatcher's voice was dispassionate. This was the way it worked. Sure, Rogue's men were probably in rotation in a one- or two-mile radius from the club. Better if I did the time check protocol with my exact location so they wouldn't come in and pull me. Otherwise, I would have a very awkward tail on my arse in the club. I recognized that it was Daisy on the line tonight. "Hey, Dais."

"Hey, Saff, how's it going?"

I paced as I spoke, anxious to get back inside.

"Good. Time check protocol."

I could hear the smile in her voice. "Response?"

"Evergreen."

"You're all good. I'll talk to you at two."

I smiled at the phone and hung up. I tried to tell myself

my brother was trying to protect me, but still, I couldn't help but feel like I was in prison.

That was a fight for another day.

I turned to go back to the club and froze when I heard the voice. "All that and you came to me."

I knew that voice. "Christ. Look, we don't need to do this."

He grinned. "I think we do. You fucking insulted me. You're not even the hot one."

So he was one of *those* dicks.

"If I'm not the hot one, why were you bothering to chat with me?"

"So that my mate could dance with your mate and shag her in the loo. I was just doing him a favor."

I had a million things that were simmering on my tongue to spew out. I did not want to make a mess. I did not want to give Gabe any more reason to not let me out. Nope. I was going to follow the rules, turn my arse around, and go back inside. "You know what? You have a good night. It's not worth it."

As I turned to go, he grabbed my arm and then tugged me back hard, his arm a steel bar around my waist as he whispered in my ear.

"Just where the fuck do you think you're going?"

CHAPTER FIVE

LACHLAN

Where did she go?

I was watching the door like a hawk… an obsessed hawk. Her mate, the one she'd pointed out, was still snogging some bloke in the corner, so she had to still be here somewhere.

Maybe she just doesn't like dancing with you.

That was bullshit. I felt it. That locked gaze, that connection, that wasn't just me. That was a real thing that had been happening.

So where did she go?

I didn't want to be that bloke, that creep who insisted on holding onto her. That was clingy. But here, I was… waiting. Like a twat. Like a fool. Like a complete and total wanker.

I sighed as I watched the door. She'd be back. I hadn't imagined that moment.

Or maybe you're out of practice.

My phone buzzed with a message from Felix telling me he'd fucked off with the blonde from earlier.

I clamped my jaw shut. *Wanker*. Of course, he dragged me out then ditched me for some girl. Bullshit.

I stole another glance toward the door before finally making a move.

The girl, the one with all the curves and the big green eyes, I'd just ask her a simple question.

When I cleared my throat, she pulled herself away from her snogging session abruptly.

She flicked me a glance and then squinted. "Can I help you?"

"I'm looking for your mate. We were dancing and she pointed you out. Said she was going to take a phone call."

The woman glanced around. "Gorgeous black woman, the kind of face that probably belonged to Nefertiti?"

"Yeah, that's her."

She smirked. "Who are you?"

I had to laugh at that. The look she was giving me said she would sever me permanently from my balls if I did anything untoward to her mate. "My friends call me Lock."

"Lock, like lock and key?"

"Lachlan."

"Right. Of course, your name would be Lachlan." She eyed me up and down. "Broody. Stupid good looks. If you're mean to my mate, I promise you I'm more than capable of being very unpleasant toward you."

I laughed at that. "Noted. Any idea where she went?"

She shook her head and glanced down at her phone. "It says she's right outside the club."

"You have a locator on your mate?"

She laughed. "Yeah, you know, us girls got to stick together."

I pondered that for a moment. "Yeah, actually, that's probably really wise."

"Do you want me to go get her? Did you upset her or something?"

I shook my head. "No, she had a phone call."

She looked down at the phone again. "Oh shit, yeah, I know exactly who called her."

I frowned at that. Not that it mattered. He'd clearly been lacking as a boyfriend if he wasn't out with her. Not to mention, she didn't touch me like a woman with a boyfriend. "Does she have someone special?"

She grinned and shook her head. "Smitten, are you?"

"Do people say that still?"

She shrugged. "I say it. And I have a ridiculous love of romantic period pieces, the whole thing. So yeah, I say smitten."

"She's all right. Smart, gorgeous, obviously, but a little locked away. But when she shows you part of her, it's like you're seeing her for the first time."

She grinned at me. "Oh, you'll do nicely."

I rubbed the back of my neck. "Right. So I'm just going to go check on her. Make sure she's good."

"Yeah, you do that. Remember what I said about those

balls of yours. Do you like them where they are? Be nice to my mate."

"Is there something about me that screams not nice?"

Maybe she can see your black heart.

She laughed at that, showing perfectly even white teeth. She was beautiful. But there was something obvious about her. Like what you saw was what you got. And while some blokes might like that, I liked a bit of mystery.

I'd always loved puzzles. Cracking them. Unraveling them.

I was probably coming on too strong, but I couldn't let go of the feeling that I needed to see her and confirm that she was okay. I had zero explanation for it. Hell, all we'd done was dance. It wasn't like she'd shared her whole life story with me. But that look she'd given me, the shy smile but blatantly honest gaze... It was hard to ignore. It was like she had seen straight into my soul.

There was no looking away, no hiding who I was, and no pretending that everything was fine, that everything was perfect. It was like she could *see* me. And that should have fucking terrified me, but all it did was make me want her more.

We're just going to see if she's okay.

That's what I told myself. That I was just going to have a quick look. What could it hurt?

Shoving through the crowd, I made a point to ask the bouncer, "Mate, have you seen a woman come through here? Black, total stunner, long braids?"

He nodded. "Yeah, she went out to the right. Do you want me to check the security cam for you?"

I shook my head. "She wouldn't leave without her mate. Thanks."

He nodded as he checked the ID of the girl who was eyeing me up and down. She gave me a warm and inviting smile.

I ignored her and pushed at the doors, nodding at a mate of mine as he was coming through the door. "Hey, Lock, what are you doing here?"

"Just heading out."

"Oh, come on, mate. I'm sure it's wicked inside."

"Sorry, I can't."

When I rounded the corner, I froze. All it took was a solid two seconds before the injection of rage into my blood sparked to life. And I released the anger I kept so tightly concealed. That motherfucker was trying to hurt her, and I was going to kill him.

Today was a perfect day for him to die.

CHAPTER SIX

SAFFRON

I PUT my hands up in front of me as if I could ward off any impending assholery with my palms. If only I had magic or something. I could still remember me at eleven, Gabe at sixteen, teasing me about how I still loved Harry Potter and how all that fantasy bullshit wasn't real. I'd never forgiven him for that actually.

"Look, I understand that you're upset." I backed up an inch. I'd walked too far from the light. Would anyone even hear me if I started screaming? I'd already put my phone away, so I couldn't send a quick text without being obvious.

I could just turn and run. The question was, how fast was he? And how fast was I in my heels?

"You were a right cunt to me in there."

I licked my lips nervously. "To be fair, you were a little handsy. But you know, we're going to let bygones be bygones, okay mate?"

CHAPTER 6 | 35

If it was strict hand-to-hand, I wouldn't be worried. But did he have a weapon?

He started moving forward slowly. "You are going to apologize for how you talked to me in there."

My toxic trait was clearly that I had zero intention of apologizing to pompous twats. The problem was that toxic trait was going to get me killed one day. So I really needed to learn to shove it down or go to therapy and take care of it.

"To be fair, you *were* being a twat." Who the hell said that? Was that me?

Yup, you. So smart.

He narrowed his gaze at me. "I'm going to teach you a fucking lesson."

"You don't want to do that. And honestly, I'm thinking with your safety in mind here."

"You're a cunt. You're not even that pretty. You're only mildly attractive for a Black girl. You certainly don't hold a candle to your fucking mate."

I swallowed hard at the insult and forced myself to smile beatifically. "Ow, again. If you're going to do this, I insist that you start with some fresh insults, but you're probably not that bright, are you? Are those the only ones you found on the internet and you're trying them out?"

Way to lay low, Saff. Way to not antagonize the twatwaffle. Way to play it safe. Now we're going to get into a fight. Gabe is never letting you out of his sight again.

The rush of anger in my veins was unexpected. The fact that because of this arsehole, Gabe was going to ground me, and likely, he'd make sure that from now on wherever I went I had an armed escort.

"I promise you that you don't want to do this, because if you do, I'm going to be forced to kick your arse. And then when I do, you know, police will get involved, and my brother will be quite cross. So let's walk away from this, okay?"

"You? The only thing you are going to do is to lie beneath me and show me just how sorry you are. Even better, use your mouth. There is one good thing about Black girls; your lips always look like you're ready to suck."

I didn't even think about it. The jab landed fast, quick, and effortless. As if I'd been trained to do it my whole goddamn life.

He growled at me and launched. I side-stepped, kicked my foot up just so that my boot planted, and tripped him.

He screamed as he scrambled for purchase then hit the ground face first. The problem was he was between me and the exit to the alley now.

"I'm going to fucking kill you."

"Sure you are, and that's why you are on the ground and I'm—"

He kicked out his foot and clipped just the edge of my boot, putting me off kilter. Then he rolled over, grabbing for me, climbing on top of me, and I was in that position. The one they warn you about in every single self-defense class, in every single training class.

Never ever, ever get on the ground.

The cold fear paralyzes you. The wicked doubt will have you ready to bargain.

Luckily, Gabe had been working with me on this scenario all my life. But I had to say, all those times he'd wrestled me when I was getting a little too big-headed, thinking that I knew how to fight, he was being gentle.

This geezer was not. He was pawing at me, trying to lick my neck. I shoved the bile down by swallowing hard.

Finally, I lifted my hips with a sharp thrust and rolled over to one side, delivering my elbow to his temple as he went down.

He howled in pain. And then I rolled to the other side, stepped one foot under my bent knee, and pushed myself to my feet.

I tasted blood. He'd bitten me. Jesus Christ. Fucking hell, human bites were the worst. They were more likely to get infected than dog bites.

Also, I touched the top of my head, and wiped away blood. I hoped to God it wasn't mine. It was going to be extra difficult to hide injuries from my brother. The bloke on the ground howled, "You're a fucking cunt."

"Says the idiot on the ground. You're going to stay there. I'm going to call 999. Get you some help and phone the police. You tried to assault me."

He spat, "Do you think anyone's going to believe you?" I frowned at that, because he had a point. "First of all, a girl outside a club, wearing leather pants, and basically a sequenced handkerchief for a top, yeah."

But I had to believe that sometimes people like to do

the right thing. And besides maybe this would make him think twice about attacking the next girl.

I moved past him quickly toward the exit, and then he grabbed for me again.

He was faster than I thought, quick on his feet. He slammed me up against the wall, and I could feel the pinpoint of a knife against my neck. The howling fear began to attack my mental functionality.

"Oh my God."

"You're not so smart anymore, are you?"

I swallowed hard. "You don't want to go to jail tonight. Are you really going to kill me?"

His eyes were full of rage, having gone completely dark. "I'm not a murderer. I don't hurt women."

"Then what the fuck do you call this?"

"*This* is your fault. If you'd just been nice..."

I clamped my jaw shut. *Do not antagonize him*. This was bad. This was very bad. And I could feel the press of his erection against me, hard, insistent. I wanted to vomit, but I wasn't going to get that luxury today.

He leaned in. "If you were just fucking nice. I was being nice to you. Of all the women in there, you had my attention and you threw it away like I was nothing." He leaned even closer. I could smell the stench of liquor on his breath and his sweat. It was bitter, acrid, and it was swirling around me, trying to invade like some kind of alien parasite.

"Be nice now and I'll make it not hurt."

I waited until he was close enough as he leaned in,

inhaling at my neck, and a shudder of revulsion snaked up my entire body. Closer. Closer.

And then I bit his ear, clamped down tight and held. He tried to yank it back, making his own ear tear, and he growled, clapping his hand over it. I held on and he dug the knife just a little tighter on my neck.

With his body trying to angle away, I had a little room. I delivered a knee strike. Sharp. Insistent. Deadly. When he didn't fully drop, I delivered another one followed by an elbow drive up under his chin. And this time after I delivered my blow, I twisted and snaked my arm around his neck, held him there, and delivered two knees to his groin. It was only then he sank down, the knife clattering on the cobblestone pavement. I inhaled sharply, stumbling away.

Was he dead? He groaned on the ground, and I got my confirmation he was still breathing. And as I stumbled toward the opening of the alley, a shadow of a man appeared.

With a yell, I staggered backward, nearly falling down.

"I see you rendered me useless."

Then I realized it was him from the bar. Lock.

"I— He— Th-that guy…"

Suddenly, Lock was on me. His enormous hands wrapped around my upper arms, gently but firm enough to keep me standing. "Fuck, you're bleeding."

And then he looked past me to the arsehole on the ground. "I'm going to fucking kill him."

I wrapped my hand into the front of his shirt. "He's already down. I just need to call 999."

"Fuck, I'm sorry. I shouldn't have let you come out here by yourself."

"No, I— Oh God, I just need to find my mate so I can leave."

He studied me closely. "You're not okay."

"No, I'm fine. It's just a little blood."

"It's not *fine*. He needs to pay for this."

I reached in my back pocket and pulled out the asshole's wallet. "I have his name. I can report him."

Lock gave me an unusual mile. His gaze still burning hot and intense, he looked desperate to stride over to Adam Paul's still prone body.

I tugged on his shirt, forcing his attention back on me. "I'm okay. I'm okay, all right? Please."

"I'm just going to have a brief chat with him," he growled.

I tugged him to me. "No. Leave him. He's not worth it."

"He put his hands on you. I promise, killing him is worth it."

"Look, do we want to spend time together or fuck with him?"

With a sigh, he nodded. "Okay, we need to get you cleaned up."

"It can't be that bad." I felt fine, but I did notice the trickle of blood.

"It is. You're bleeding." And then he examined my neck. "You're bleeding from the neck too. Did he do that?"

"He got fancy with a knife."

"Fucking hell. I'll kill him."

Fury surged in his eyes when he glanced at the idiot on the ground, and I stopped him again. "I'm fine, Lock, I just… I can't go inside. I need to text Tabs and tell her to meet me."

"Come on, you're coming with me."

I hesitated for a moment, pulling back. "No, I— Tabs, I want to go to her and get cleaned up. Spend the night."

"I'm going to get you somewhere safe. We're going to clean you up, and then we're going to text Tabs. That's her name?"

I nodded. "Tabatha."

"Good, then we'll text her and tell her where you are, okay?"

I shifted on my feet. This was not the plan. Then again, getting jumped in an alley outside the club was not the plan, and Tabs was having fun. And all my instincts told me Lock was not like that bloke, so I nodded. "Where are we going?"

"I live not far from here."

"Oh, of course, your place."

He released me briefly to pull out his wallet and then he pulled out his license. "Here you go. Text Tabatha now. Tell her you're with me, yeah? That way she'll know where you are and you'll feel a little safer."

I lifted my gaze and studied him. "You really are a good bloke, yeah?"

He shrugged. "Well, that's debatable, but right now I'm trying to get you taken care of."

"You know I can take care of myself, right?"

He laughed. "Yes, you have rendered me useless in defending you. But please allow me to be of *some* service. My ego can only takes so much."

I had to laugh at that. "Fine." I took a photo of his license and sent it to Tabs.

Saff: *I'll explain later. I'm fine.*

And then I handed him back his ID.

"Excellent. Now, can you walk?"

I frowned at him. "Of course, I can walk." That was the truth. *Mostly* the truth, because I hadn't exactly accounted for the adrenaline flooding my veins. I took a step forward, and in the heels I may have wobbled slightly.

Lock's firm hands wrapped around my upper arms again. "That's what I thought."

And then the giant oaf bent down, picked me up, and the threw me over his shoulder as if I weighed nothing.

"You're coming with me,"

CHAPTER SEVEN

SAFFRON

"So, is this the serial killer den?"

Lock laughed as he eased me down just outside his door so he could pull out his keys. He slid the heavy steel door on its track and then stepped aside. "Ladies first. Or can you not walk?"

I shook my head. "I can *walk*. You didn't have to carry me *all the way* here."

"It's only three streets over."

"You know what I mean."

I liked his loft. It fit him somehow. I barely knew this bloke, but I knew that his place somehow *fit*. The trim was a mix of wood and steel, some chrome, but there were eclectic pieces of art from what looked like all over the world. A mismatch of paintings and artwork on every surface. A couch that looked comfortable and lived in.

"I like your place."

He gave me a nod. "It was mine and my brother's for

when we were in the city or stopping through. But it's mine now."

I frowned at his word choice. "You said it *was* yours and your brother's."

He licked his bottom lip. "He died. Five years ago."

I winced. "Shit, I'm so sorry."

"It's all right. I guess. That's supposedly the right response you're supposed to give people. I miss him every day."

"It must have been a special relationship for you guys to be able to share a place together."

He shrugged. "Yeah. Charlie was the best."

"Lachlan and Charlie?"

He shook his head laughing. "Lachlan and Charleston. If you can imagine that."

"Oh my God, your parents."

"Oh yes, just as pretentious as you would believe they would be." He indicated the bathroom. "Just through there. I'll grab the first aid kit and meet you there."

"You don't have to do all this. I'm fine."

"You keep saying that. I'll determine if you're okay. Did you hear from your mate?"

"I love that you know Tabs already. She texted back. She said she will sever you from your balls if you hurt me."

"Of that, I have little doubt."

His bathroom was the sort of thing you saw in *Architectural Digest*. Clean and modern. But instead of the proverbial white that was the style of all modern bathrooms these days, it was all black and grays, and the effect was gorgeous.

He had one of those sauna steam showers, and all I wanted to do was jump in.

The floor was that wood looking tile, ceramic, I think. It was beautiful. The backsplash was all shimmering browns and golds with a really ornate enormous mirror. When he joined me, he indicated the chair at the vanity. "Take a seat."

"This is ridiculous. I'm fine."

He also had a T-shirt he offered. "Something to change into. You probably got some blood on yours."

I glanced down at my top which was mostly a shimmering metallic panel on the front and some strings. The top was entirely backless, and once I let go, my breasts would be screaming for freedom. The top was free of blood, but it would be nice to cover up a little more. I was too exposed.

"Thank you."

"All right, let's see about this." He grabbed the alcohol and the iodine and made a quick work of starting to clean me up.

I hissed and jerked back when the alcohol touched my skin. "Ow."

"Sorry. No one told you to be a badass today."

"I'm basically a badass every day."

His smile was soft. "I don't doubt it. Your mate said that you were celebrating tonight. What were you celebrating?"

I gave him a sheepish smile. "It's my birthday."

"No shit. Well this is bad. I didn't even get to wish you a happy birthday properly. You need cake."

"No, I don't."

"My mum always said a birthday is not a birthday without a cake. I think we can get some ordered."

I shook my head. "That's really un—"

He already had his phone out and was texting. "The cake will be here in ten minutes. There's a bakery down the way. They're on one of my food service apps."

"Well, isn't that convenient?"

"They're certainly handy. You didn't want to celebrate with your family?"

It was my turn to go somber. "My parents died two years ago."

He cursed under his breath as he put the remnants of the gauze and bandages away. "Fuck."

"Yeah, fuck."

"What happened?"

I chose the cover story. "Plane crash."

He winced. "Fuck, I'm so sorry."

I left out the part about how there had been a bomb on that plane specifically designed to kill them and only them. The madman had figured out who they were and took them from me deliberately. Intentionally.

I also left out the part about having full intentions of finding that madman one day and annihilating him off the face of the earth. Those were the kinds of things you didn't say to a stranger.

"Did they do anything for your birthday when you were little?"

I nodded and smiled. "Yeah, there were two things we always did. Dad always made sure that for my birthday, he would teach me a new skill. Something he expected me to master by my next birthday. Sometimes there was a puzzle. Sometimes it was a martial arts thing. Sometimes it was learning to play a really complicated song. He always said an Abott should be multitalented. He was the best. And Mum she always shared a journal entry she'd written for me when I was a baby. Sometimes they were silly, sometimes they were poignant. But we'd snuggle in bed first thing in the morning and she'd read it to me. I guess she started it when she was pregnant with me."

"You guys were close then?"

I nodded. "Yeah. I get the sense when I wake up sometimes that I can almost hear them."

He nodded. "That happens to me all the time with Charlie. Especially being here. I can't count the number of times I could swear any moment I would walk out into the kitchen and he'd be standing there doing a proper English fry up. He loved a fry up."

"How did your parents take it?"

"The same way that they usually do. Distanced themselves. Became detached."

"So, what are we going to do while we wait for the cake?"

"You tell me," I said, my voice husky.

"I have a great puzzle."

"A puzzle?" Had I heard him right?

"If you were some other woman, I would go into lewd detail about all of the dirty things I could do to you."

The gut punch robbed me of air. "Oh," I said, ducking my head.

He used a finger to lift my chin up and force me to meet his gaze. "But because you're you and have me so twisted in knots my hands are shaking with the need to touch you, I'll keep all my dirty fantasies to myself... for now."

CHAPTER EIGHT

SAFFRON

An hour later, I winced at the clock. "I should go."

He stood immediately. "Where are you going?"

"I don't know. I feel like I should just go."

I didn't *want* to. Which was part of the problem. He was smart. And funny. And I liked him, but I was not the hookup kind. Besides, if I didn't turn up at Tabatha's, Gabe was going to lose his shit. "I just have to go."

"Just stay a little longer. You haven't even finished your cake."

"You're right. And it is a good cake."

"Yeah, it is."

The truth of it was, I couldn't think of a good enough reason to stay other than I could see the danger here. The danger for me. The way he watched me with intensity. I could feel his gaze on me with every step I took. The way he made the hairs on my arm stand up… I wanted more of that. I wanted more of *him*. I wanted his attention on me. I had dismissed him at first as a carefree playboy. But he was more than that. The more he talked about his brother, the more I was able to talk about my parents. And he listened. He offered no reproach. Just listened.

"Finish your cake. Then I'll walk you back to your mate's place. You said she's near here, right?"

I nodded. "You've already done too much."

"It's your fucking birthday. You should celebrate."

"You know I can't finish the rest of this, right?"

"What about another fork? We can share a fork, or maybe I can just lick the frosting and you eat the cake."

I stared at him. "Eww."

"Oh, come on. I don't—"

"Uh-uh, no, we're not doing that."

"Come on," he said, laughing.

"Licking frosting is like sharing toothbrush."

He laughed. "You mean to tell me you've never shared your toothbrush with someone you're dating?"

I shuddered. "No. I tend not to have relationships that last that long. But also, *ewww*."

He laughed. "Oh, come on. You're putting toothpaste on the brush, right? So it's already getting clean."

I shook my head. "No. No, no, no."

He just laughed. "I've got a toothbrush in there that you should use to brush your teeth before you go."

I shuddered. "No. Gross."

I knew he was fucking with me.

He relented and stood up and got himself another fork before joining me on the couch.

"Which birthday is this?"

"Twenty-two. In the States, that would have some big significant meaning. Not too much here."

He laughed. "Right. But it's still your birthday. You should still do something to celebrate."

"My brother will pull some family dinner on me tomorrow. There will be more cake. Although, he never seems to listen when I tell him that I'm not twelve and I don't want an ice cream cake anymore."

"What's wrong with ice cream cake?"

"I don't know. They're great sometimes, but I can't eat a whole one."

"Well, it's your birthday, so you should have whatever kind of cake you want."

"Agreed." I scooped up another forkful of cake.

"So what's your brother like? Do you still live with him?"

I nodded. "He is *overprotective*." It was the nicest word I could think of.

"If you were my sister, I probably wouldn't let you out of the house either."

I rolled my eyes. "What's that supposed to mean?"

He laughed and then leaned back on the sofa, one arm casually placed against the back edge. "Besides you being well fit? And men being twats?"

"Whatever the hell that means."

"Oh, come on, you must know."

I shrugged. "Know what?"

He eyed me up and down. "You're clearly a stunner."

I shrugged. "I don't feel like one."

"What do you mean? Other blokes you're dealing with must be blind."

I laughed. "You are very good for the ego, Mr. King."

"I have eyeballs. My eyesight is not compromised."

"Yes, I see you do. And they are a very pretty color."

"Hold on. It's *your* birthday. I give *you* the compliments."

"By all means, please do." I laughed.

He studied me then. "You're taking the piss, right?"

"About what?"

"About blokes not fancying you."

"I didn't say that. But the blokes that fancy me, most of them can't seem to take not being fancied back. For the last two years I've been in the haze of grief and school. I haven't really had time to focus on anything like relationships, so I don't really date much."

"That's bullshit."

"Are you hitting on me, Mr. King?"

He nodded enthusiastically. "Yes, a hundred percent."

His honesty made me laugh. "I'm not your type. I promise you."

His gaze narrowed. "And pray tell, what is my type?"

Shit. I cleared my throat. "Look, you are obviously, uh, very attractive."

He lifted a brow. "Oh, I like where this is going. Keep talking."

"The way you zeroed in on me at the club, you don't ever have to approach someone. But the ones who intrigue you aren't the ones that are more obvious. And you clearly like a challenge."

He cocked his head and smiled. "You stared first."

When I stuck my tongue out at him, he continued. "Suffice it to say you're beautiful, smart, and you have this hidden quality to you. A part you keep far away from everyone else. You don't show it, but I could see it. The moment our eyes met, I could feel it. I think you sell yourself short. You are impossible to look away from. Most women I know act coy and turn away. But *you*... You made me work. You don't look away. You don't hide from hard things. That's exceptionally sexy. You are clearly clever, and you can kick arse with the best of them. You don't see yourself clearly enough because you're comparing yourself to Tabs. Is she beautiful? A hundred percent. But what you see is what you get. She's open. You are an untapped well of emotions. More complex."

The way he was looking at me made my skin prickle as the heat radiated from my body. "I don't do hookups," I blurted. "I need to know someone. Like them. Trust them." *Christ*. I was so nervous my mouth was running away from me.

"Who says I'm looking for a hookup?" His voice was low, husky, and tempting.

"I am here in your flat. You didn't kill me yet, so…"

He sighed and leaned forward with his elbows on his knees. "You are beautiful. Like I said, I like to work for things. Everyone assumes that I want things easy. I don't.

My whole life, people have given me things without giving me the opportunity to work for them."

"You want to work for me?"

"I'd like a shot," he said with a smirk. "And to start, that means I can't assume. So I'm good with some work."

I swallowed hard, studying him. "People do that a lot, don't they?"

"What's that?" he asked.

"Underestimate you."

"Tell me if you want to go, and I will take you to your mate. Do I want you to stay? Yes. Do I want you? Undoubtedly. Do I want to work for your trust? Yes, I think I like it better that way."

Oh boy, I was so dead. Men like him were dangerous, because with the intensity of his gaze, the way he was watching me, I believed him. Or at least I wanted to believe him. Every instinct told me he was telling me the truth. Which worried me because I already wanted him.

What's wrong with that?

"So who are you? What makes you tick?"

He licked his lips. "Oh no, you don't. This is your birthday. We are focusing on you." He jumped up. "Come with me."

"What are you doing?"

"Oh, just come here." He walked me over to a bureau just to the right of his kitchen, pressed buttons on the keypad, and the door slid back, revealing a massive entertainment system. One of the shelves slid out and an actual honest-to-God record player slid out.

I laughed. "Of course, you've got a record player."

He rolled his eyes. "You're missing out."

On the bottom were rows of albums. When I looked down, I saw that there was an intricate shelving system, album after album, and I laughed. "I see a lot of rock classics here."

He grinned. "Yes, but my favorite is Stevie Wonder. Do you like Stevie?"

"He's classic. 'Superstitious' is bloody brilliant. You must love music."

He took my hand and twirled me. "We, my dear, are going to finish our dance we started at the club."

I laughed. "You can't be serious."

"Come on." He pulled the Stevie Wonder album out of its sleeve and placed it on the record player. And as Stevie's voice rang clear, Lachlan King held out his hand. "Come on, are you going to have a little fun on your birthday or not?"

"Who are you?"

"Lachlan. We met at the club? Try and keep up."

I laughed. I knew he couldn't know my mother had loved Stevie. So much so that it was my middle name. I didn't tell Lachlan that though. Instead, I stared down at his hand.

"It's your birthday. You deserve to dance on your birthday."

"You are correct, Mr. King."

"I hope you know that every time you say it like that it sounds just a little bit dirty."

"What? No. I'm not being dirty."

He laughed. "A little bit. It's *how* you say it. I don't know what to tell you. You are sexualizing me, and I'm not sure how I feel about it." His voice took on a husky note.

I coughed a laugh. "Oh my God, you're impossible."

"Well, I just call it like I see it."

I rolled my eyes. "Maybe this is how you lure all the women. Bring them up here, play them a little Stevie Wonder, dance in the living room with them. Perfect date situation. Is this what you call work? You're going to have to do better than this," I teased.

"No other women. This is my sanctuary. Besides, Charlie and I had a rule. No randoms in the flat, because randoms tended to want to come back for more. And once he had this girl who stalked him. She came to the house because he hadn't called."

I laughed. "Oh no."

"Oh yes. My mother had a lot to say about that. So when we moved in together here, we made a rule. No randoms."

"Am I random?"

"Absolutely not. You are the kind of girl who makes me work. Hence, not a random."

"Smooth, Mr. King, very smooth."

"Now, Miss Abott, take my hand."

And I did. He was warm and solid. For the first time in too long, I trusted someone. It was that easy.

"Now be a good girl and tell me how you like to be touched."

CHAPTER NINE

SAFFRON

I should get up to leave. I should. After dancing and laughing and being fed, not only did I feel completely cared for in a way that was odd and strange from a perfect stranger, I knew I liked it. Which was problematic at best, and it wasn't like I could keep it. There was no worry or doubt that could happen. This was a distinctly temporary arrangement, so I needed to get up and go.

It doesn't have to be temporary.

I thought of Gabe going all big brother on him. Where is your family? Where did you come from? What are your financials? All of those things that would scare off anyone.

There was no way. Lock was exactly the kind of bloke who would *not* pass muster. Besides, tonight was a perfect night. It was the kind of night that you wished and hoped for, but I needed to get back to Tabs.

What if for once, you didn't talk yourself out of something amazing? What if for once you stayed?

I couldn't. It was too complicated.

Or maybe you're scared to stay. Scared of loving someone and losing them again?

Oooh, my self-awareness was on the warpath today.

"You want to leave." He sighed.

I froze and then turned in Lock's arms, the warmth of them surrounding me. His clean pine scent enveloped me, tempting me to stay where I was.

We'd fallen asleep on the couch watching *Luther*. And it had been the most perfect night.

"You've done enough. You cheered me up and provided first aid. I should go."

His gaze searched mine, and I could feel the erratic thumping of his heart beneath my hand.

"If you want to go, let's go. I'll walk you. Better yet, maybe a cab. How far is it?"

I rattled off the address. "But I can walk. It's no big deal. I don't want to bother you."

He lifted a brow. "First of all, I'm going with you. Second of all, it's cold. Come on, let's get you going."

I knew that was my cue. Except when he shifted and pulled me closer so he could roll us over, I realized I didn't want to leave. I was enjoying the cocoon of his arms. I liked him. I liked the way I felt. I liked the way he held me. I liked it all. So why was I so eager to run?

His voice held a low chuckle. "You're not getting up, Saff."

"I don't want to," I whispered. For once I wanted to be reckless.

The corner of his lips tipped up then. "Then why are you going?"

"Because I think I *should* be going." For some reason, it was easy to be honest with him instead of finding the half-truths that I was always telling for survival.

"What if you just did what you wanted?"

I licked my bottom lip. "I don't know. I have never done that."

"I dare you to do what you want tonight, Saff. Tell me. Be honest." His voice had gone husky, pitching even lower, quieter, more intimate. "What is it you want to do? I know what I want to do, but I'm going to need you to tell me because I want to make sure I've got it right."

I wanted to tell him. I wanted to be the kind of woman who could be daring and just say the words.

His voice was low. Barely above a whisper. He angled his nose toward mine, gently brushing them together. His lips never touched mine, but his breath was a caress. "Tell me what you want. Do you want to get up and leave my arms and walk out the door? Or do you want to stay? Nothing has to happen. I can just keep holding you until morning."

My pussy had a lot to say about it. *Bitch stay. If you leave, I will kill you.* I felt the question in my bones. I did *not* want to leave here. "I want to stay."

A slow smile spread over his lips. "Excellent. So you'll stay. Why don't you text Tabatha?"

I rolled over and grabbed my phone and fired off a text.

When I was done, his finger lightly played with one of

the slim braids that framed my face. "These are so small. It must be a bitch to put in and take out."

I nodded. "I go somewhere and have it done. I have a particular set of skills, but it doesn't include braiding."

"They're beautiful. You look stunning with them."

"Lock?"

His voice was low as he murmured at me, "Hmm?"

"I want you to kiss me."

I watched as his tongue peeked out to touch his bottom lip, and his teeth scraped along, chasing his tongue.

His hand reached up and cupped my face. "You're fucking beautiful. I saw you in the club, and you were so open but guarded at the same time. The challenge in your eyes was like a beacon. You looked like you were trying to be happy for someone else. And it made me want to know why you were guarded, why you were sad, why you were bothering to pretend for anyone. When you met my gaze, you weren't guarded at all. I could tell you were hurting about something. There was this locked in spark. I felt like I could *see* you, the real you. I think that for the real you, a club is the last place on earth you wanted to be. Yes, you like to dance, but you'd rather do it at a party with friends than at a loud club full of anonymous strangers. I can see the real you who is scared to disappoint anyone. You are desperate to prove that you belong even though they should be the ones proving they are worthy of you because you are a fucking a queen and I can see it. It's simmering right there. Just under the surface. And every time there's a flare of it, you tamp it down, make it smaller, hide it."

I tried not to shift under the scrutiny and the discomfort. Lachlan King had seen too much, and I wanted to shake him off. I tried to duck my head, but he gently slipped a finger under my chin and tilted my head up so I was meeting his gaze once again. "Don't hide from me now."

I shook my head, blinking tears back. "You don't even know me."

"Oh, I see you. And I'm fucking desperate to touch you."

I smiled up at him, feeling the odd thrill of having him see me so clearly when nobody else did. "So, are you going to kiss me or not, Mr. King?"

The corner of his lip pulled up in a smirk again, and his gaze dipped to my lips. "It depends."

"On what?"

"If you think you're ready."

"Oh, I'm ready. I can handle whatever you dish out."

His chuckle was low and throaty, and I wanted to bask in that laugh, that cocky, knowing laugh. His grip tightened in my hair.

As he brought his lips closer to mine and hovered just over my lips, his voice was soft. He whispered, "I'm never going to be the same." And then the jolt of electricity hit me hard as our lips brushed, sending an electrical charge through me.

The first kiss was soft. A warning.

The next was an exploration as he pressed firmer and his tongue chased over my lips. And then when I gave him access, I heard him moan and curse low. Then I knew exactly what he'd meant. I was in a whole heap of trouble. This wasn't any ordinary kiss. This wasn't some random thing that could be walked away from. This was something I was going to feel soul deep tomorrow. Lachlan King could kiss. Worse, Lachlan King could own my soul if I let him.

His tongue was seeking. Exploring. When I parted my lips to let him inside, he gave me an appreciative grunt, and then delved in, fully exploring, taking his time, finding all the nooks and crannies and what made me groan. He put everything into one kiss, into one taste, into making sure that if it was the last one he was ever going to get, he was going to do it thoroughly.

All I could do was hold on for dear life as my hands slid up into his hair, my nails scouring his scalp and me trying to angle my body closer, tighter into his.

Somewhere between Lachlan's lips pressing over mine and his tongue staking its claim, he rolled on top of me and settled between my thighs, the motion bringing the length of his erection against me, and I gasped.

Lock tore his lips from mine, his eyes glassy and unfocused as he groaned. "Fuck, I love the way you taste."

I nodded. "I—" I swallowed hard. "Y-your dick is... wow."

He choked out a laugh and dropped his forehead to mine. "Talking dirty to me already."

I laughed. "You're huge." It was the truth.

"You are certainly good for my ego."

I really needed a muzzle. "Something tells me, with an erection like that, you don't have an ego problem."

His chuckle was raspy as he brought his lips back to mine. "Fuck, I want to keep you."

The way he said it, I wanted to be kept. God, was that an option? Could I let him keep me?

I didn't care. Right now, I didn't want this to stop.

Lachlan was more careful now, angling his hips away from mine so he wasn't putting the full force of his weight on me. "Fuck, you're so beautiful." He dragged his lips along my jaw, onto my neck. "Your scent, it's been driving me mad all night. What is that?"

"I wish I knew. It was my mother's."

"I'm going to find out what that is and buy bottles of it."

He was welcome to try. Hell, I had tried. His nose ran up the column of my neck, and then his tongue traced along, following the path. "I want to eat you whole."

"I'm yours," I whispered.

The words and grunts that followed next, I couldn't remember. All I knew was that Lachlan's hands were almost as skilled as his mouth. His hands slid into my hair, gentle with my braids but still applying pressure to my scalp as he angled me, his mouth guiding back for more. I learned that he could kiss for hours. Make it his whole damn meal.

The more impatient I grew for him to hurry the show along, the longer he took, savoring me, tasting me. When I started to move my hips, seeking the heat of his erection, he hissed in my ear. "Fucking hell, I know. I know. I feel it too. I just... I want to take my time."

I groaned in frustration then, and he laughed. But when I slid my hands up under his shirt, he helped me to take it off.

And then we were a scramble of limbs. I tossed the T-shirt he'd given me quickly. When he pulled at the knot holding my top in place, I frowned at it when it did not give.

I reached for the knot and gave it a gentle tug. With a little maneuvering, it broke free easily. "I was worried there for a second."

And as he stripped the glittery sequins away from me, he groaned. "Jesus Christ, your tits are bloody fantastic."

The way he stared, I felt beautiful and wanted. I don't think anyone had ever looked at me like that before.

"Are you okay with this?"

"Yes, I'm okay. Just don't stop touching me."

His answer was a groan as he dipped his head to kiss my nipple.

I understood right away why he was asking if I was okay with all of this, because when Lachlan King wrapped his mouth around my nipple, I felt the level of his intensity. It was as if the man was trying to swallow me whole.

His big hands molded over my breasts. And as he took one nipple in his mouth, he sucked as much of my breast as would follow slowly inside. With the other hand, he squeezed and teased the other nipple, plucking gently.

And then my head was thrashing on the cushions of the couch. "Oh my God, Lock."

He switched to the other nipple, this time angling his body so he was lying on top of me. I shifted down further so his face was at nipple level.

My hands tugged on his hair, trying to pull him closer. With a soft chuckle, he moaned against my breast. When he finally released my nipple, I was panting, needing more.

His gaze lifted to me. "Can I taste you?"

I frowned. He *was* tasting me. Then his raised brow told me what he meant. Oh God, yes. I couldn't really make a coherent thought though, so what I did was moan enthusiastically. He chuckled. His hands slid down to the top of my leather leggings, sliding down deeper under the elastic of those and my knickers.

When his fingertip found my drenched pussy, he cursed against my skin. "Oh Jesus Christ, you're so wet already."

"I— I didn't know I could—"

Lachlan held perfectly still with his mouth over my nipple, and I could feel his warm breath as he inhaled jagged breaths. Slowly, he eased back from my nipple and lifted his head to meet my gaze. "You're tight. Fuuuck."

"I'm sorry. I-I just need to relax."

He shook his head. "Shh, I'll help you relax. That's my job. Don't apologize. Everything about you feels fantastic. Bloody brilliant."

"Lock, I need—" I couldn't even string words together.

I squeezed very deliberately around his finger, and he

cursed again. "Fuck, Saff. You're going to kill me. I have to taste you first. I just need—"

"Yes. God, please, just—"

"Okay, okay, bossy."

I had to laugh at that. I'd never once laughed during sex. Usually I was concentrating too hard, or focused on relaxing, trying to enjoy myself. And because of that, maybe I wasn't in the moment. But this... Lachlan was... Oh God.

With rough strokes, he shifted his weight and then started to peel down my leather leggings.

"Your arse looks amazing in these, just so you know."

I giggled as he tugged them past my knees, and my knickers with them. His double concentration was so strong I almost had to laugh. He was so intent on his task.

When I was fully naked in front of him, his gaze raked over me as if he was unsure where to look first. "I'm going to eat you whole." One hand was on the open fly of his jeans, palming and adjusting himself. What I found fascinating was that he didn't fully take it out. He wasn't eager to have it touched. Instead, he left it in the confines of his pants, depriving me of the view. I groaned at that.

He gave me a lopsided smile that I'd already come to cherish. "We'll get to that. Trust me, we'll get there. I just want to be able to focus. And if he's out, he's going to try and run the show. I want to know what you taste like before I basically lose my last brain cell."

I had to laugh at that. I was pressing my thighs together now, trying to help alleviate the ache, because God, I was desperate for something. Anything.

His big hands scooped my arse then, lifting me easily and scooting me up to the head of the couch. I squealed at the movement, which helped me spread my legs for him. But apparently, he wanted them wider apart because he spread them even further, his gaze on my inner thighs intent. "I want to put every part of you in my mouth, but we'll take our time later, okay?"

I nodded urgently. "Yeah, okay."

"You are going to be the death of me, you know that?"

"You talk a lot."

And then he laughed. It was low and throaty, the best sound in the world. Like drinking hot chocolate next to an open fire on a really cold night. I wanted to encapsulate that feeling forever.

But Lock had other plans because he didn't want warm. He wanted fiery, blazing, inferno hot.

He leaned down then, turning me so one leg was over one end of the couch and the other on the floor, and I was completely open and bare to him. Automatically, I brought my hands down to cover myself, and he caught my wrist. "No. You're stunning. I fucking mean it. Do you understand me?"

I swallowed and nodded. I understood, but it didn't mean I wasn't self-conscious. But when he started kissing up my inner thighs, I forgot about being self-conscious and mostly was trying to will him to go higher.

I did not have to will him to, though, because he was just as obsessed with it as I was. With each kiss, he brought himself closer to my center. And then he ran his tongue from my opening to my clit and moaned deep, as if he was eating his favorite ice cream. In slow motion he kept using the flat of his tongue, licking as if I was an ice cream or a popsicle. I threw my head back, my hands on his hair, trying to force him to hurry up. God, what was that feeling?

It almost felt like he was laughing as he devoured his meal. But he was thorough. When his tongue started to slide into my sex deeper and deeper and he moaned as he ate, I couldn't help it; my leg started to automatically draw in around his ears and he used his hands with a firm press on my thighs to keep me open.

He lifted his head, his eyes nearly feral, his voice barely more than a growl. "You try and close your legs again, and I'll stop my meal. Unless you don't want this anymore."

"Oh no, I want it."

"Good girl. Now lay back and let me eat."

A shiver ran up my spine and I couldn't even believe this was me. And then when he introduced a finger as he was sucking on my clit, he watched me carefully. This time there was no resistance. His fingers slid right in and he closed his eyes, moaning and humming, making me shake. God, I was so close to… something. So close.

When he started really sucking on my clit, I knew. His finger was delving inside, and I slid my hands into his hair, pulling him into me, my hips wantonly riding his face.

With his other hand, he grabbed my arse and held me up slightly so he could have more of me. Oh my God. I was going to die just like this, naked and splayed on Lachlan's couch. Because surely the only thing that could come after something this good was death.

The slam of the orgasm hit my spine so hard I almost choked as I cried out, "Oh my God, Lachlan."

All he did was muffle something appreciatively against my clit. But it washed over me, over and over, the waves of pleasure hitting me as my back arched and my head fell back on the cushion. But Lachlan didn't stop. He kept lapping at me, fucking me with his fingers.

I tried to push his head up, but he opened his eyes and his gaze locked on mine as he shook his head.

"I don't… I don't know if I can."

But apparently I could, because he flicked his tongue over my clit, and that sent another wave of pleasure through me.

This time, my legs did lock around his head. My hips lifted, and I screamed. Lachlan released me then with a shit-eating grin on his face as I was panting like I'd just run a goddamn marathon.

I didn't know what to say or do. All I could do was lay there because every muscle in my body was limp, exhausted, wrung out.

Lock smiled down at me and pressed a solitary kiss on my clit. Gently. "That's my girl. You did so good. I'm going to give you a minute to recuperate, and then we're going in for another round."

That forced my eyes open. "What?"

"Oh, you didn't think we were done, did you?"

"Wow."

"Hopefully that's a good thing."

He was serious too. With his jeans hanging unbuttoned and low on his hips, he bent down and picked me up easily as if I weighed nothing. He carried me through the living area then upstairs, and I could only presume it was leading to the loft. "You're taking me to your dungeon?"

"Yes, my red room of pain."

I must have frowned a little, because he laughed. "I'm teasing. I'm taking you to my bed. I think you'll be more comfortable."

I nodded. "Yeah, comfortable. That's the word."

He laughed, brushing my lips with his. "Do you have any idea how good you kiss? I don't think I'll ever get enough."

I clenched just thinking about him with his mouth on me. Where in the world did I find him?

Once he laid me in his bed, he did strip out of his jeans. His boxer briefs clung to his rigid erection. He palmed himself but still didn't take his boxers off. He climbed on the bed next to me. "Are you all right?"

"Yeah. But, um, the two orgasms didn't include one for you."

"Oh, only two? I can do better."

I laughed at that. "Oh my God. Men like you exist? It's not even fair."

"Yes, men like me exist. Now move over. I want to hold you."

And that's all he did. He slid into bed, tucking me close and angling his hips away from me.

Frustrated, I frowned and tried to sit up. "Will you let me touch you?"

He shook his head, tried to pull me closer, and kissed my forehead. "Because you're small and you barely took my fingers, I'm going to need all my control."

When my hand wrapped around his stiffness, he groaned low. "Oh my God. Fuck, Saff…"

"So big," I moaned.

"Oh God, your hand feels so good."

I squeezed more. Curious now, I shifted my position so I was kneeling next to him on the bed. And then I hooked my fingers in the elastic and tugged down.

"Fucking hell, Saff."

"Yes, Lachlan?"

"You don't…"

I turned my full attention on the thick erection in front of me.

I didn't venture to think how big he was. All I knew was that I had never been with anyone *this* big. Jesus. That was going to be a hell of a tight fit. But instead of a frisson of fear or trepidation, my pussy clenched in anticipation.

But I wanted him. That was easy and clear for me to understand. I wanted him, so I was going to try.

When I wrapped my fingers around the base of him, his hips lifted ever so slightly off the bed.

"Lachlan…"

His response was strained. "Uh-huh?"

"I've never really done this before, so I need some help."

His eyes opened. "Oh God, you don't need to."

But I was already moving. I wrapped my lips around his tip, running my tongue around the underside of his dick as his hands went to my hair.

"Oh my God, Saff. I don't think I can take it."

I released him. "Am I doing something wrong?"

He shook his head vehemently. "No. You're not doing anything wrong. Don't stop. Oh, no wait. Actually stop. I'm not going to make it."

"Which is it?"

"I don't know. This is torture."

I frowned down at the thickness in front of me. "Is it actually torture?"

He laughed. "Oh my God. Where did I find you?"

"Tell me what to do."

"Oh God, yeah, just lower your head onto him slowly."

I did as instructed, using my hand at the base to keep him steady, wrapping my mouth around the mushroom-shaped tip, sliding down to the ridge. I used a little teeth and he hissed. "Oh my God. Fuck me."

His hips shoved up, and I got more than I'd expected. I moaned in surprise, but still took the additional inches.

He coughed. "Oh God, sorry. Wow."

And then I just started moving, using my hands as well as my mouth.

Every now and again he moaned with some instruction along the lines of, "Yes, use your hands. And tighter."

So I clamped my hand tighter around him or tightened my mouth around him. And then his hands went to my hair, keeping me in position. But then he quickly released me, pulling me away from my new toy.

"Fuck. Stop, stop, stop, stop."

I immediately released him. "Did I do something?"

"Yes, you gave me the best fucking novice blowjob of my life, and I am so close to coming, but I want to be inside you."

I absently stroked him. "Um, yeah, let's try it."

He eyed me dubiously. "We don't have to. This? This has been more than enough. You are—"

"Lachlan," I met his gaze, "I want to try."

He reached into the nightstand for a condom. As I lay back on the bed, I watched him intently, my tongue still licking my bottom lip. "Jesus Christ, if you keep looking at me like that, I'm going to come before I'm inside you."

"What?"

"You're beautiful. I'm keeping you."

And a part of me wished he could. When I didn't answer, he leaned forward and pressed a soft kiss to my lips as he lay between my legs. "I'm going to kiss that sweet cunt of yours because I miss your taste."

In seconds, he had my breath hitching and me calling his name. I didn't think I'd be able to have more orgasms, but all it took was his expert mouth and it was as if my body was already tuned in, already marked by him, knew that call of his. I readied myself.

He notched himself at my slick entrance and nudged forward. Yup, he was big.

But I wasn't uncomfortable. It just felt... full. He

leaned forward, pulling one of my nipples into his mouth, gently grazing it with his teeth. And as he suckled, making my back arch, he drove forward some more. He did a gentle pull back, a retreat that made me hiss. The friction was... exquisite.

My hips moved automatically. I wanted him. My hands scratched along his back trying to pull him deeper.

"Stop, love. I..." He gasped. "Need..." A groan escaped. "To go..." He cursed. "Slow."

"I'm sorry. I just... I need more."

"Fuuuck." He drew back and then slid all the way home with a grunt.

That's when I stopped breathing.

It didn't take long for him to start moving. Incrementally at first, then those short strokes became long ones. Lachlan pulled back, bracing his arm next to my hip, watching me. His other hand caressed my face, moving one braid of hair to try and tuck it behind my ear. "God and Jesus Christ, you feel so good. You are so tight. So soft. So fucking hot."

His hand that had been gently pulling on my hair moved to my hip, adjusting my leg and drawing it up higher on his hip. He picked up the pace, his hands squeezing my arse, pulling me into him. And I hung on for the ride. When a thumb found my clit and started circling it as he pounded into me, the last orgasm that I didn't know I had in me came barreling through, tightening every limb and sending shock waves through my body.

Lachlan cursed as he dropped his face on my neck,

pounding deep strokes, retreat, stroke, retreat, thumb on my clit, rubbing circles. "Fuck. Fuck. Fuck," was all he whispered into my neck, and then he was roaring my name. "Fuck Saff, Saff, Saff…"

Then another orgasm surprised me, rolling through on his last short, digging stroke. Lachlan's hands grasped my arse tightly, and he came with the guttural grunt of my name on his lips.

My arms were too limp to wrap around him, but he rolled me onto my side to face him. "So we're clear, your pussy is fucking perfection. It's also mine for the foreseeable future. Get comfortable with your legs open because I plan to be between them a lot."

I swallowed hard and nodded. "Okay then."

He kissed my lips softly, rolling away. He went into the bathroom to secure the condom and then came back with a warm wet washcloth to help me clean up. He was back in bed with me in no time and pulled me to him. "Come here. Let's go to sleep. Get some rest. Because we're doing that again."

CHAPTER TEN

SAFFRON

I ached.

From my toes up to my pussy. The sweet ache between my thighs was all I could think about when I woke up with the early morning light streaming in. Everything ached.

Lachlan hadn't given me much rest last night, but he had been very thorough about sex. I wasn't sure my pussy was going to survive the day. Walking was going to be difficult.

Last night after the second time, he'd gone to get me water and an ibuprofen, ostensibly because we'd had a bit to drink, but that pain reliever was coming in handy this morning, and when I tried to stretch, it didn't hurt that bad. I just had that low thrumming hum in my vagina. Like I had been up to no good.

You have and we liked it.

God, I liked him, and that was really, really dangerous.

I needed to find my phone.

I was as quiet as I could be, sneaking around his bedroom. None of my clothes were up here, but I did manage to swab some toothpaste over my teeth and tongue and found a washcloth to wash my face. And then I snuck downstairs.

I knew what it looked like.

It looked like I was running away. And I wasn't running *exactly*. I was walking. It wasn't like I wanted to go. I wanted to stay. I was so tempted to let him make me breakfast. To maybe go for another round.

But in the early hours before dawn, I could see how my brother would react to this. I could see him losing his shit. Last night Lock was everything I needed. But my life, the craziness of it, I'd had to keep him in the dark. *Lie*. And he already saw too much. Lying to someone like him was not going to be easy. He would demand answers that I couldn't give, and he would eventually leave.

Or maybe you could just give it a shot. Get more sex. And maybe you just tell him that you have one of those jobs that you can't tell him what you do. Maybe he'll be okay with that.

I glanced around at my surroundings again. The rich details, the furnishings, the artwork. He was the kind of bloke who would ask questions. He wouldn't be comfortable being in the dark. I couldn't keep him.

Finally dressed again in my walk-of-shame outfit, I found my phone and texted Tabs.

Saff: *On my way to you.*

Tabs: *OMG. Get your slutty arse over here and tell me everything!*

I checked the time. It was barely four o'clock. I'd be smart and get a car.

I was so tempted to go back upstairs. Even knowing that was a bad idea.

Maybe if you can't kiss him, at least leave a note so he's not worried.

Right.

I was just going to leave him a quick note because I didn't want him to worry. I could hear the bullshit in my own thoughts. I *wanted* him to find me again. But that was a terrible idea.

If he came looking for me, Gabe would have several very large men end his life.

But I couldn't *not* say anything. So I found a piece of paper and a pen on the coffee table and scribbled a note. *Thank you for the first aid.* And then leaving my shoes off, I tiptoed back upstairs, which I knew was a risk, but still. I left it on the nightstand on my side of the bed then tiptoed back down the stairs. I found my shoes, and with one last look, I let myself out.

Outside of his building, my car was already waiting. I had to resist the urge to run back upstairs and throw caution to the wind and give no fucks, because that wasn't my life. I didn't do things like that. I didn't have one-night stands with strangers. And I sure as hell didn't have relationships with strangers. There was no way this could work between us. It was just untenable, and I needed to see that.

And if I dicked around anymore with his emotions, he was likely to end up maimed or dead. Everything would be better if I just stayed the fuck away. So sadly, I gave the driver Tab's address and walked away.

Forever.

Leaving was the only way to protect him and my heart.

CHAPTER ELEVEN
LACHLAN

THE HARSH STREAKS of early sunlight jarred me awake. Next was the scent that had me rolling over into full consciousness. Perfume. Rose. Maybe lilies? Vanilla? Something else. What was that?

Considering I never brought anyone back here, where had it come from?

I reached over to the other side of the bed, and it was cool to the touch. But the scent grew stronger. I took another whiff, inhaling deeply, letting my lungs fill with it, letting it permeate my skin. And then I remembered. *Saff.*

Jesus Christ.

That had me sitting straight up in bed, the sheet falling to my waist. Okay, so much for rules being broken. "Saff? Are you in here?"

I didn't hear the shower or anything in my bedroom, but I'd showed her around last night to the other room. Maybe she hadn't wanted to wake me?

I had zero compunction about climbing out of bed and letting my morning wood swing in the wind. After all, I'd been gifted for a reason. Might as well show it off.

"Saff? Where are you?"

I rubbed my eyes, trying to clear them, somehow sure that once I cleared out the sleep I would find her, maybe sitting at my breakfast bar? What the hell?

You know what this is. She ghosted.

There was no way. Last night hadn't been some casual hookup thing.

Maybe not for you.

No. Fucking hell, no.

I hurried down the stairs into the other bedroom on the first floor, sure I would find her there.

But nothing. No Saff.

She clearly wasn't there. Nothing was disturbed. Hell, the door wasn't even open. I went into the bathroom to double-check, even though I knew she wasn't there.

I grabbed a towel and wrapped it around my waist, suddenly less interested in my morning wood swinging in the wind.

Fucking hell.

She had fucking ghosted me. Such bullshit.

Maybe she left a note?

At that point I figured it was wishful thinking, because if she'd snuck out in the middle of the night, or in our case, very early in the morning, there was no way she left a note. But one could always hope.

Sure enough, no note in the kitchen or the living room.

My mood was decidedly sour until I saw the slip of paper on the nightstand.

My ego restored, I jogged over and snapped it up, ready to find a phone number, email address, something. But no. Instead, in the most perfect calligraphy-type penmanship I had ever seen, were the simple words, *Thank you for the first aid.* And I could do nothing else but slump back onto my bed.

How had that gone so wrong? Last night had been real. I hadn't imagined that.

But Jesus, she'd really fucking ghosted me.

That sharp, possessive side of me was irritated, because we'd had fun. More than fun. She'd come several times. And we'd had real, honest-to-God conversations. So where the fuck had she gone?

I laid back on the bed, irritated with myself. Irritated with her. Reminding myself that I was not going to go back to the club and search the cameras for her face ID and then make a call or two to a dodgy mate who might be able to get facial recognition and help me find her. Because even I had standards.

Except that was exactly what I wanted to do. Drag her back here and keep her in bed for a week. See if she wanted to leave then.

Possessive much?

Fine. I heard a scrape back downstairs, and suddenly hope crashed into my chest. Fuck, she hadn't left. She'd gone out to get breakfast. Aww, well done, love.

This time instead of letting everything flap, I stopped by

the closet, got a pair of boxers, and shoved them on. I grabbed a T-shirt because of the morning chill. And despite my determination to look nonchalant, I hurried down the bloody stairs. "Saff, Jesus, I thought you'd left. Not that I was stalking you, or—"

No Saff. I paused at the end of the stairs, frowning. Something was off. Everything looked the same, but something was not quite right. And then I felt it. The hairs pricked on the back of my neck. There was movement behind me, not on the stairs, but in the powder room to the right.

I shifted my feet to the left automatically, and there was someone dressed in black, masked and everything. Jesus fucking Christ, it was like something out of a Bourne movie. I shook my head. "Mate, I don't have any money here. You can take whatever you want, but leave the art on the walls, for fuck's sake. That's a Sebastian Winston. But the rest, take them. Wait, leave the Xander Chase one too, and the Z Con. But you can take everything else. I have no quarrel with you."

He's not here for things. He's wearing a mask. He's here for you.

My brain took a moment to go on a quick vacation because, what the fuck? My whole life I'd had anti-kidnapping and basic self-defense training as well as some martial arts.

So I didn't even back up. And then on my periphery, coming from the second bedroom, I saw Jason Bourne number two. Oh, fuck. Was that Aaron Cross? Honestly, I'd rather fight Aaron Cross. He wasn't nearly as badass as Bourne, but this was bad.

I put my hands up. "Mate, easy does it. We don't have to do this."

The one in front of me cocked his head, and I couldn't tell for sure, but under the mask, I almost thought he smiled.

The one coming at me from the bedroom, was moving more briskly, like he meant fucking business.

Okay, maybe that was Bourne, and maybe the other one was Cross. Either way, this was bad.

The one on the left grabbed for me. I ducked and threw out a punch. It connected, and he staggered backward. And then, Jesus Christ, did he growl?

Bourne came for me full tackle. I only managed to block one of his punches, but then… *Shit.*

I took one straight to the nose. The pain exploded behind my eyeballs, and a siphoning crunch had me nearly gagging as I staggered backward but stayed on my feet.

All I could do was block. Which was useless. I tripped, sending me backward into the kitchen and around the counter. My knives, my knives. Where the fuck were my— Fuck, they were in the drawers. That was not going to work. All I could manage was to grab the cutting board which I held up as a shield and whacked the other one on the face with it. Oh yeah, that hurt. Nice oak chopping board.

I planted it on his face again and delivered another punch, which also hurt my hand. Jesus fucking Christ. But he grunted and actually went down to his knee. When he was down there, I delivered a kick to the balls. I almost wanted to apologize because as a bloke, I knew how that felt.

Cross, or Bourne, whichever one it was, came at me. Why didn't they have guns? Why weren't they going to shoot me?

They don't want to shoot you. They want to take you.

And with that realization, I started really fighting for my life. I took several more hits, but I stayed mostly on my feet. But then, a third one came from upstairs. Fuck, had he been in my bloody bath?

His voice was low, like it had been through a cement mixer. "Stop fucking about. Bag him."

Bag? Oh, hell no. I wasn't getting black bagged and dragged off to some godforsaken place for a fucking ransom. "Mate, you're not going to get any money out of my folks or my grandfather. Oh fuck, are you SAS? About the princess, that wasn't my fault, mate. I didn't know—"

Something pierced my shoulder and I frowned down at it. It wasn't a bullet. It was a dart.

Immediately, my tongue started to swell. It felt like I was suddenly under water. I could move, but only very slowly. And I took another punch to the face, which... Fuck, that hurt.

And then, the worst happened. A black bag slipped over my face, and that bright sunlight that had woken me not thirty minutes ago, faded to black.

To be continued in The King…

Thank you for reading THE HEIR! I hope you enjoyed the first book in my GENTLEMEN ROGUES series.

What's worse than a gorgeous one-night stand who doesn't remember you? Having to pretend to be his wife…For **work**.

We just got our newest recruit at Rogues Division…Lachlan King, the sexy billionaire playboy who seduced me into one night of wild, soul-shattering, sex.

When I slipped out of his bed three months ago, I never expected to see him again. But now, I have to pretend to be his wife.

Read The King Now!

It was all for show. At least it was supposed to be. When I agreed to be Jaya Trudeaux's fake fiancee for her sister's wedding, I didn't expect to crave her like I do. After all, billionaires make great dates on paper.
One-click SEXY IN STILETTOS now!

> *"Sexy in Stilettos is a **fun and flirty romance** with complex characters and a great storyline." - Amazon Reviewer*

From the moment I see her I know she's meant to be mine. I don't care if she has a boyfriend. I'm the crowned prince of the Winston Isles and I'm used to getting what I want, and I won't let the crown stand in my way.

Can't get enough billionaires? Meet a cocky, billionaire prince that goes undercover in **Cheeky Royal**! He's a prince with a secret to protect. The last distraction he can afford is his gorgeous as sin new neighbor.
His secrets could get them killed, but still, he can't stay away…
Read Cheeky Royal now!

Turn the page for an excerpt from Cheeky Royal…

ALSO FROM NANA MALONE

CHEEKY ROYAL

"You make a really good model. I'm sure dozens of artists have volunteered to paint you before."
He shook his head. "Not that I can recall. Why? Are you offering?"

I grinned. "I usually do nudes." Why did I say that? It wasn't true. Because you're hoping he'll volunteer as tribute.

He shrugged then reached behind his back and pulled his shirt up, tugged it free, and tossed it aside. "How is this for nude?"

Fuck. Me. I stared for a moment, mouth open and looking like an idiot. Then, well, I snapped a picture. Okay fine, I snapped several. "Uh, that's a start."

He ran a hand through his hair and tussled it, so I snapped several of that. These were romance-cover gold. Getting into it, he started posing for me, making silly faces. I got closer to him, snapping more close-ups of his face. That incredible face.

Then suddenly he went deadly serious again, the intensity in his eyes going harder somehow, sharper. Like a razor. "You look nervous. I thought you said you were used to nudes."

I swallowed around the lump in my throat. "Yeah, at school whenever we had a model, they were always nude. I got used to it."

He narrowed his gaze. "Are you sure about that?"
Shit. He could tell. "Yeah, I am. It's just a human form. Male. Female. No big deal."

His lopsided grin flashed, and my stomach flipped. Stupid traitorous body…and damn him for being so damn good looking. I tried to keep the lens centered on his face, but I had to get several of his abs, for you know…research.
But when his hand rubbed over his stomach and then slid to the button on his jeans, I gasped, "What are you doing?"
"Well, you said you were used doing nudes. Will that make you more comfortable as a photographer?"

I swallowed again, unable to answer, wanting to know what he was doing, how far he would go. And how far would I go?

The button popped, and I swallowed the sawdust in my mouth. I snapped a picture of his hands.

Well yeah, and his abs. So sue me. He popped another button, giving me a hint of the forbidden thing I couldn't have. I kept snapping away. We were locked in this odd, intimate game of chicken. I swung the lens up to capture his face. His gaze was slightly hooded. His lips parted…turned on. I stepped back a step to capture all of him. His jeans loose, his feet bare. Sitting on the stool, leaning back slightly and giving me the sex face, because that's what it was—God's honest truth—the sex face. And I was a total goner.

"You're not taking pictures, Len." His voice was barely above a whisper.

"Oh, sorry." I snapped several in succession. Full body shots, face shots, torso shots. There were several torso shots. I wanted to fully capture what was happening.
He unbuttoned another button, taunting me, tantalizing me. Then he reached into his jeans, and my gaze snapped to meet his. I wanted to say something. Intervene in some way…help maybe…ask him what he was doing. But I couldn't. We were locked in a game that I couldn't break free from. Now I wanted more. I wanted to know just how far he would go.

Would he go nude? Or would he stay in this half-undressed state, teasing me, tempting me to do the thing that I shouldn't do?

I snapped more photos, but this time I was close. I was looking down on him with the camera, angling so I could see his

perfectly sculpted abs as they flexed. His hand was inside his jeans. From the bulge, I knew he was touching himself. And then I snapped my gaze up to his face.
Sebastian licked his lip, and I captured the moment that tongue met flesh.

Heat flooded my body, and I pressed my thighs together to abate the ache. At that point, I was just snapping photos, completely in the zone, wanting to see what he might do next.

"Len..."
"Sebastian." My voice was so breathy I could barely get it past my lips.
"Do you want to come closer?"
"I--I think maybe I'm close enough?"
His teeth grazed his bottom lip. "Are you sure about that? I have another question for you."

I snapped several more images, ranging from face shots to shoulders, to torso. Yeah, I also went back to the hand-around-his-dick thing because...wow. "Yeah? Go ahead."
"Why didn't you tell me about your boyfriend 'til now?"
Oh shit. "I—I'm not sure. I didn't think it mattered. It sort of feels like we're supposed to be friends." Lies all lies.
He stood, his big body crowding me. "Yeah, friends..."
I swallowed hard. I couldn't bloody think with him so close. His scent assaulted me, sandalwood and something that was pure Sebastian wrapped around me, making me weak. Making me tingle as I inhaled his scent. Heat throbbed between my

thighs, even as my knees went weak. "Sebastian, wh—what are you doing?"

"Proving to you that we're not friends. Will you let me?"

He was asking my permission. I knew what I wanted to say. I understood what was at stake. But then he raised his hand and traced his knuckles over my cheek, and a whimper escaped.

His voice went softer, so low when he spoke, his words were more like a rumble than anything intelligible. "Is that you telling me to stop?"

Seriously, there were supposed to be words. There were. But somehow I couldn't manage them, so like an idiot I shook my head.

His hand slid into my curls as he gently angled my head. When he leaned down, his lips a whisper from mine, he whispered, "This is all I've been thinking about."

Read Cheeky Royal now!

ABOUT NANA MALONE

USA Today Best Seller, Nana Malone's love of all things romance and adventure started with a tattered romantic suspense she "borrowed" from her cousin.

It was a sultry summer afternoon in Ghana, and Nana was a precocious thirteen. She's been in love with kick butt heroines ever since. With her overactive imagination, and channeling her inner Buffy, it was only a matter a time before she started creating her own characters.

Now she writes about sexy royals and smokin' hot bodyguards when she's not hiding her tiara from Kidlet, chasing a puppy who refuses to shake without a treat, or begging her husband to listen to her latest hair-brained idea.

COPYRIGHT

This is a work of fiction. Names, characters, places, and incidents either are the product of the author's imagination or are used fictitiously, and any resemblance to actual persons living or dead, business establishments, events, or locales, is entirely coincidental.

The Heir

Book 1 in the Gentlemen Rogues Series

COPYRIGHT © 2022 by Nana Malone

All rights reserved. No part of this book may be used or reproduced in any manner whatsoever without written permission of the author except in the case of brief quotations embodied in critical articles or reviews.

Cover Art by Minx Malone

Edited by Angie Ramey and Michele Ficht

Published in the United States of America

Printed in Great Britain
by Amazon